DRAGON STORM

Erin and Rockhammer

DRAGON STORM

Erin and Rockhammer

ALASTAIR CHISHOLM

nosy crow

First published in the UK in 2023 by Nosy Crow Ltd
The Crow's Nest, 14 Baden Place,
Crosby Row, London SE1 1YW, UK

Nosy Crow Eireann Ltd
44 Orchard Grove, Kenmare,
Co Kerry, V93 FY22, Ireland

Nosy Crow and associated logos are trademarks
and/or registered trademarks of Nosy Crow Ltd

ISBN: 978 1 83994 222 8

A CIP catalogue record for this book is available from the British Library

Printed and bound in Great Britain by Clays Ltd, Elcograf S.p.A.

Papers used by Nosy Crow are made from wood grown in sustainable forests.

1 3 5 7 9 10 8 6 4 2

www.nosycrow.com

IN THE LAND OF DRACONIS, THERE ARE NO DRAGONS.

Once, there were. Once, humans
and dragons were friends, and guarded
the land. They were wise, and strong, and
created the great city of Rivven together.

But then came the Dragon Storm, and
the dragons retreated from the world
of humans. To the men and women of
Draconis, they became legends and myth.

And so, these days, in the land of Draconis,
there are no dragons...

...Or so people thought.

ERIN

Erin stood inside a wide circle of sand, with her sword high and her shield ready, and waited for her enemies.

A figure stepped into the circle and faced her. He was shorter than Erin, and thinner, but he looked quick and dangerous. She let him move forward, keeping her feet steady, waiting...

He lunged!

...And missed, his sword swishing past

as Erin swayed to the left. She brought her own blade round in a short tight arc, and he yelped and fell. Erin steadied herself as the next attacker stepped forward. This one was more cautious, holding back and keeping his guard up. His eyes were hostile, but he looked nervous. Erin *roared* and rushed at him suddenly, and he stumbled backwards. She swung her shield up and knocked him flat.

Then came a thin quick girl, her face tight and careful. She parried Erin's first attack and stabbed, and Erin scrambled back as the tip of the sword whistled past her face. Erin drove forward, slipped to one side in a feint and then back, smashing her sword hilt against the girl's. The girl cursed and dropped her sword, and Erin struck again.

The last attacker approached. He was different. Wide-shouldered, almost as tall as Erin, he held his sword well, and confidently. Like her, he stepped carefully, his shield up and his sword ready.

Erin struck, but he caught her blow on his shield and heaved, shoving her back! She gasped and staggered as he pushed forward, and she almost fell, before getting her balance and striking back. They pulled apart and circled each other warily. Erin's sword and shield were heavy. Sweat trickled down her forehead, and the back of her tunic was damp. She would have to end this soon…

She moved to the side, and then struck again, fast!

Again he caught the blow on his shield, and again he heaved, but this time she was ready. As he pushed forward, she dropped her own shield, grabbed the top of his, and *yanked* it towards her. He gave a shout of surprise and dragged himself back, and she let his momentum carry her round behind him, twisting, swinging her sword and stabbing against his back.

"Touch!" came a voice, and the boy sagged to his knees.

"Hah!" he gasped out. "Nice trick. Thought I had you."

Erin grinned and stood up straight. Around them, the others cheered. Tom, her largest opponent, was grinning and rubbing his back, where Erin's wooden sword had hit. Around them were Connor, Ellis and Cara. Ellis and Cara were smiling, though Connor looked annoyed. Outside the circle, Mira and Kai cheered.

They were in a training ground surrounded by other training areas, a racecourse, and a few small buildings, all sitting inside a vast underground hall. It was a colossal space, and yet for these children, and for the adults who taught them, it had become like home.

For this was the Dragonseer Guild Hall, and Erin and her friends were *dragonseers*.

Daisy, their self-defence teacher, stepped into the ring. "Well done, Erin!" she said, beaming. "At this rate we'll have to try two against one!"

Erin and Rockhammer

Erin laughed. "Bring 'em on!"

Daisy chuckled. "Careful now. That last move of yours cost you your shield — one more attacker and you'd have been in trouble."

Daisy was short and cheerful, with blonde hair tied in a ponytail that bounced as she walked, and bright yellow leggings and top. Erin sometimes thought she didn't look

much like a warrior, but she had fought enough practice sessions to know that Daisy was the best. She took her job seriously, because the Dragonseer Guild had a serious purpose.

The hall was hidden away somewhere under the city of Rivven in the land of Draconis. Above them life went on as normal, but down here … things were different.

As Erin watched, Tom closed his eyes and concentrated, and a shape appeared behind him.

It was twice as tall as Tom, with a long neck, dark-red skin like iron in a forge, and orange-and-yellow stripes stripes of flame. She was a dragon, and her name was Ironskin.

"Hello, Tomas," she said, leaning down and

resting her head against his. "Are you all right? You took a hit there."

Tom leaned against her and smiled. "It's all right, Ironskin," he said. "They're just wooden swords." He winced and rubbed his back again. "Still sore, though. I wouldn't want to fight Erin with a real blade!"

"Well done, Erin!" said Ellis, her first opponent. He was a pretty good sword fighter, but he was much more interested in exploring and map-making. Cara, the third opponent, inspected her wrist where Erin had smashed against her sword hilt.

"Sneaky," she muttered. She looked as if she was making a note for next time. Cara was a careful, clever girl. Her dragon,

Silverthief, was quite small, not much bigger than Cara, but she was fiercely protective and now she glared at Erin.

"You did it!" said Mira, running up to her. Mira was hopeless with a sword and had been knocked out of the competition early. She preferred tinkering with machines, and her dragon Flameteller, with his bronze colours, looked a little like a machine himself.

"How can you run *towards* them like that?" Mira asked. "Aren't you scared?"

Erin laughed. "It's easy when I'm fighting. I don't think about it!" She turned to Connor, her second opponent. "Good match," she said, grinning.

Connor scowled. "It was supposed to be

a *sword* fight," he complained. "You hit me with your shield!"

"Still counts," said Erin. "Never mind, I'm sure you'll win *one* day…"

"Perhaps we should try something else," he said with a sour smile. "What about a summoning contest?" He clicked his fingers, and his dragon Lightspirit appeared. Lightspirit was a thin, wispy creature, with pale green brows.

"Where's *your* dragon, Erin?" asked Connor in a mocking voice.

Erin's face went red, but before she could

answer, Daisy stepped between them.

"Enough of that!" she snapped. "Erin won fair and square, Connor – you were too timid, and she used her advantage. Now, it's Mr Creedy's class next, and you'll all need your dragons with you. Erin, you can go to Drun and get him to help you. You others, head over to the training grounds. Well done, everyone!"

The others headed across, but Daisy called Erin back.

"There's a sword competition next month," she said. "They have a junior section, and I think you'd do very well. How would you like to take part?"

Erin grinned. "Yeah! Here in Rivven?"

Daisy smiled. "No, it's in Strick, but I could take you, if you'd like?"

Strick was the next town along the coast. It was only a few miles away, a morning's ride by cart, but Erin hesitated. "Maybe," she said at last. "I might be busy."

Daisy looked surprised. "Really?"

Erin looked away. She felt suddenly hot. "Um, I have to go see Drun for help summoning Rocky."

"Erin?"

"I have to go see Drun now!"

Erin walked away quickly, leaving Daisy gazing after her in surprise.

ROCK-HAMMER

Drun's hut was round and made of stone, with a chimney and two huge doors. The doors were open and Drun was inside, tending the fire. He was wearing his usual leather jerkin, his face hidden under a great grey beard, and he beamed when he saw her.

"Mornin', miss!"

Erin smiled. Drun knew the names and details of every dragon he'd ever met, but he often found humans hard to remember.

Erin and Rockhammer

"Good morning, Drun," she said. "I'm here to summon Rocky."

He nodded. "Come in! The fire's almost ready."

Erin entered and sat. Drun sat across the flames from her.

"So," he said, "still havin' problems summonin' then?"

DRAGON STORM

The world of dragons was very different to that of humans. Drun called it a world of *ideas*. But a few special humans could reach across, connect to one dragon and invite them back to the human world. Erin was a dragonseer, and like the other children she had a special dragon. He was named Rockhammer, and she loved him more than anything ... but there was a problem. No matter how she tried, she couldn't form the connection by herself.

"The others make it look so easy," she complained. "Connor just *clicked his fingers*!"

"Never you mind him," said Drun, smiling. "Everyone struggles till they get the knack of it. And you *did* summon him once, didn't you?"

Erin bit her lip and nodded. "I suppose."

The flames in the fire grew tall, and Drun's face drifted in the smoke. "Tell me about it," he said softly.

Erin thought back. "I was at the foster home," she said. "I hadn't been there long. It was nice."

She remembered it. Her new foster parents had owned a small inn, and she had been tucked into a tiny room too small for guests. It was cramped, and the window let in draughts, and her feet poked out of the bottom of the bed … but it was the first room she'd ever had of her own, and she loved it.

"It was at night," she said quietly. "There was a wild storm – the whole house was shaking! And I was looking out of the window…"

DRAGON STORM

The storm had rattled the windows, shaken the chimney pots, made the walls creak and groan like a ship at sea, and Erin had lain huddled under her blanket, and had seen...

"Eyes," she whispered. "Peering in the window, too big for a bird, or an animal..."

Drun murmured under his breath, and the smoke curled into a shape – a creature with a strong head and a ridge of spikes. Erin smiled.

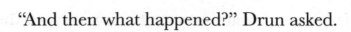

"And then what happened?" Drun asked.

Erin hesitated. "Then the house fell down," she said.

Drun laughed, and Erin grinned. "No, really! Lightning hit the chimney, and the wall exploded! The roof caught fire, the bricks split, and everything crashed down…"

"And that's when Rockhammer appeared?" Drun asked.

Erin nodded. "Suddenly he was there, in the room. He was all squeezed in, but he was there, and he held the roof up." Erin smiled. "He saved me."

She shrugged. "No one else saw him. When they came to rescue us, he was gone. But the next day, Malik came round." Malik was the king's clerk, but secretly he worked for the Guild, finding potential dragonseers. "He told my foster parents there was an apprenticeship space for a clerk. They didn't want me to go, but they knew it was best, and the inn was out of business until they rebuilt it, so…"

"So you joined the Guild," said Drun, smiling.

Erin nodded. In the smoke she could see Rockhammer, and hear his voice in her head, warm and strong.

Hello, Erin!

"Remember that feeling," said Drun. "You're goin' to complete the summoning, Erin – ready?"

Erin started. "What? No! No, I can't, you know that!"

"It's fine," he said in a soothing voice.

"Rockhammer's nearly here, you just need to guide him…"

But Erin trembled, and the smoke wavered in front of her. "No, I can't do it!"

"Easy…"

Erin?

"No!" She backed away from the fire, and the smoke collapsed. Her heart was thumping, and she felt suddenly sick. A horrible rush of electricity ran up the backs of her arms, and she couldn't stop shaking.

Drun sighed. "Nearly, that time. It's all right, lass. Here, calm down – we'll try again."

"Don't tell me to calm down!" she snapped, "And don't try to *trick* me! I can't do it, understand?" She folded her arms round her body tightly.

Drun frowned at her in surprise, but then he smiled and shrugged. "O' course."

He took her through the steps again, and this time, as the creature in the smoke appeared, he stayed with her. And this time the flames burned higher and higher, and then died out all at once…

In the darkness something moved.

Erin turned, and there he was – the largest of all the children's dragons, mighty and powerful, with a huge ridge running down his back, and dark colouring like rain against a slate wall. His legs were huge and sturdy, his face fierce.

Erin and Rockhammer

"Rockhammer!" she cried, hugging him.
He lowered his huge head down to hers.

"Hello, Erin," he rumbled. His voice was
like boulders grinding together. "Hello,
Drun."

DRAGON STORM

"How are you, my lad?" asked Drun.

"Feeling strong," growled Rockhammer. "Perhaps I'm getting my power!"

Drun laughed. "You're already strong!"

"Maybe I'm getting *stronger*!"

Every dragon had a special power, something incredible. It didn't come right away, and the young dragonseers often wondered about what it might be. Some already had theirs – Ironskin could make a shield, Pathseeker could see through illusions. Kai's dragon, Boneshadow, could even heal broken bones. "No one knows what it will be," Drun liked to say, "but it'll be somethin' you need, and it'll happen when you need it." The children had all agreed, though –

when Rockhammer's power came, it would be something *ferocious*...

They left the hut and Erin turned back.

"Thank you," she said to Drun. "Sorry I got cross. I just—"

Drun waved a hand. "Not to worry. We'll get the hang o' it." He studied her. "Do *you* know what the problem is?"

"No," she said, and Rockhammer shook his head too.

Drun frowned. "Ah, well. See you tomorrow!"

They headed back to the training ground.

"How did the sword fight go?" asked Rockhammer.

Erin laughed. "I won! Connor was so cross."

The dragon grinned, showing all his teeth. "Daisy wants me to enter a competition, but it's in Strick, so I said no."

"No?"

She squirmed. "You know I don't like to go too far. I like it here."

"Hmm," rumbled Rockhammer.

Erin shook her head to clear her thoughts. "It's good to see you, Rocky."

"You too! Do you think you'll be able to summon me yourself one day?"

Erin shrugged. "Maybe. Hey, let's catch the others up."

Rockhammer nodded, and they trotted to join the rest.

Erin bit her lip. She felt bad about lying

to Drun. The truth was, she knew why she couldn't summon Rockhammer. But she couldn't tell anyone – not Drun, not the other children, not even Rockhammer, her best friend in the whole world…

In fact, *especially* not Rockhammer.

SENT AWAY

Back at the training ground, Vice Chancellor Creedy was waiting.

"When you're *quite* ready," he said in an icy voice.

Erin felt her face flush. "Sorry, sir."

Creedy, the second in command at the Dragonseer Guild, was thin, dressed entirely in grey, and looked annoyed all the time. Kai had once described him as looking like he was chewing a wasp.

"Well," he said, "now that we're *all* here, we will practise hovering – exactly three metres above the ground. Begin!"

The children scrambled up on to the backs of their dragons, but Creedy bellowed, "STOP!" He glared at them. "These are not *horses*," he snapped. "These are *dragons*. They are your dragons, but you are also their humans. *Ask* before you clamber all over them! Work together!"

Erin stopped and smiled. "Sorry, Rocky," she said. "May I?"

Rockhammer grinned. "You may," he said, lowering his head. Erin put her arms round his neck and he pulled her up.

The dragons each found a space and

stretched their wings. Some were better at flying than others. Tom and Cara's dragons, Ironskin and Silverthief, managed easily, but Ellis's dragon, Pathseeker, only had stumpy wings, and lifted up and sank down, flapping furiously. Rockhammer's wings were thick and muscled, and as he flapped them the dust flew up from the training ground.

"Careful!" said Connor from beside them. His dragon, Lightspirit, had a long, thin body, twisting like a snake, and short stubby wings. They flapped almost too quickly to see, and her tail lashed around to keep her steady. She was drifting towards them.

"*You* be careful!" said Erin.

Creedy called, "Watch your position, dragons!"

"It's *you*!" hissed Lightspirit. "You're *moving*!"

"No, *you* are!" snapped Rockhammer. "You're too close. Get away!"

The little dragon was almost within touching distance now, her tail still thrashing. Erin felt a sudden wave of panic. She didn't like it when people got too close. She didn't like to be hemmed in. It was a hot, trapped sensation, and it made her feel as if she was in a fight, or like a sharp red fire was burning through her, until suddenly—

"Get AWAY!" she screamed, and then

reached and shoved Lightspirit with her foot.

Lightspirit spun. "You kicked me!" she yelped.

"You're too *close*!" Erin shouted.

Connor was furious. "Leave Lightspirit alone!" he roared. "And get your stupid dragon away!"

"He's not stupid! Don't you *ever* say that!" Seeing red, and hardly even thinking about what she was doing, Erin scrambled to her feet, still on Rockhammer's back, and leapt through the air, colliding with Connor!

Lightspirit reared in terror. "What are you doing?!" she yelped, twisting her neck as Erin and Connor wrestled above her. "Stop! I can't take the weight! Stop!"

She spun once more and then collapsed, and Connor and Erin crashed down hard on to the ground.

"Ow!"

"Argh!"

From where she lay, Erin looked up and saw Rockhammer's worried face.

"Erin?"

But then Creedy pushed in front of the dragon, his face purple with rage.

"Come with me, *now*." he hissed.

Later, Erin sat in Berin's office.

The Lady Berin was the chancellor of the Dragonseer Guild. She was a kind person, and Erin liked her. But today she looked serious. She sat at her desk and studied Erin. Behind her stood Creedy.

"Connor says you kicked Lightspirit," she said. "Is that right?"

Erin scowled. "She was too close! It was Connor's fault!"

"And then," said Berin carefully, "you leapt, in mid-air, from Rockhammer's back on to Lightspirit's, and attacked Connor?"

"It wasn't like that!" protested Erin.

"It was *exactly* like that, child!" snapped Creedy.

Berin raised a hand. "Why?" she asked mildly.

Erin shrugged. "Connor's so *mean*!" she muttered. "He's always making fun of me because I can't summon!"

"Hmm." Berin looked down. "Do you have any idea why that is? Drun says there might be something…"

Erin shook her head.

"Hmm," said Berin again.

"These are strange times," she said at last. "The dragons are returning for the first time in a thousand years. But other forces are gathering. Someone is holding a dragon prisoner right here in Rivven."

Erin knew this. She and her friends had discovered it – a wild dragon, quite unlike the others, was being held in a dungeon of the Royal Palace and kept there by magic. And the children knew who was keeping him there…

"It's the king, isn't it?" she blurted.

Berin and Creedy looked surprised.

Erin said, "We figured it out. King Godfic is really a dragonseer, isn't he?"

Berin hesitated. "Perhaps," she said at last. "And if so, then a crisis is coming and we must be ready."

Erin looked at her. "Do you mean a war?"

"Yes," said Creedy, but Berin shook her head.

"*No*," she said firmly. "Not if I can help it."

Creedy pursed his lips but said nothing.

Berin continued. "But to *stop* a war, I have to know I can count on my dragonseers to stay calm, whatever happens." She sighed. "Erin…

This isn't the first fight you've been in. You get angry quickly. You act without thinking. This isn't *working*."

Erin ducked her head. Her face was hot and tears pricked her eyes. *This isn't working.* She'd heard that before. At foster homes, in the orphanage, after fights or accidents or arguments... Her hands balled into fists. *This isn't working.*

"Mr Creedy has a suggestion," said Berin. "There's a place, outside the city, where they know about dragons. It is run by –" she smiled – "by someone I trust. There is something there that might help."

Erin's heart sank. "I don't want to go," she whispered. "I'm sorry. I'll be good. Please

don't send me away!"

Berin seemed surprised. "Erin, we're not throwing you out! You're one of us. But this place may help – you can stay as long as you need, and return whenever you like. Don't you want to try?"

Erin hesitated. "Just me?" she asked. "On my own?"

"I have some research to do there," said Creedy. "And Drun will accompany us – perhaps you can finally learn how to summon your dragon. Connor will be my assistant."

Erin gasped. "No! Anyone but him!"

"*Yes*," said Berin firmly. "Connor's good at research; he's the right person to help. And…" She shrugged. "Erin, you two have squabbled since the day you met, and today someone could have been seriously hurt! Connor *will* go, and you two *will* learn to get along. Understand?"

Erin sank her head. "Yes, miss."

She tried to feel hopeful. Berin seemed sincere. But Erin knew the truth. She was being sent away, like she had been before.

Because *this isn't working*. Because she got angry. And if she couldn't stop getting angry...

They would never let her back into the Guild.

STILLNESS

They set off early the next day.

Drun collected Erin while the soft glowing lights inside the Dragonseer Guild cavern were still low, like morning stars before dawn. Together they summoned Rockhammer, and the huge dragon rubbed his cheek against Erin's.

"Good morning," he growled.

Erin smiled. "Hey, Rocky."

Then Drun led them to the storerooms,

down the steps to the lower chambers, and on to a small dock beside an underground canal.

The Dragonseer Guild was hidden from the world. To the people of the city of Rivven, and the land of Draconis, dragons were a myth, tales of terror for dark nights. One day, Berin said, the dragons could show themselves – but not yet. So the Guild stayed hidden, with only two ways in or out. One was a maze of twisting, moving passages, the Clockwork Corridors, that led to a hidden lane in the city. The other was this underground canal.

Creedy and Connor were at the dock already, silent and waiting next to a small barge.

"Mornin'!" called Drun cheerfully.

Creedy gave them a brief nod.

DRAGON STORM

"Good morning, Drun," said Connor politely. He ignored Erin, and she ignored him.

Drun grinned. "Ready for adventure then?" He gestured to the barge. "In you get. Humans only, ha!"

Erin turned to Rockhammer and stroked his neck. He nodded, and faded out of sight, but he wasn't completely gone – they were still connected, and she could hear his voice in her head.

Erin and Rockhammer

Still here!

Erin smiled.

The children climbed in, and then Drun and Creedy. Drun cast off, and then, using a long pole, pushed them upstream.

The canal ran through an underground tunnel, and the only light was a lamp at the prow of the boat. The boat rocked gently, and Connor gripped tightly to the sides, his face pale. Erin didn't mind the water, or the motion of the boat, but the silence bothered her. There was only the shift of Drun's pole, a dripping from the roof and the echo of lapping water.

It's all right, said Rockhammer's voice.

Erin tried to stay calm, but the barge

was tiny, and everyone was pressed close together – too close. Erin's skin prickled, and her stomach growled in dread. She wanted to get out, but she couldn't—

"Here," said Drun suddenly.

Erin looked up and realised he was offering her the pole. "Take this, will you?"

She took it, and Drun showed her how to punt the boat through the water against the gentle current.

"Nice and steady," he said in a friendly voice. "Nothin' to it. Girl with strong arms like yours, why am I doin' the work, eh?" He laughed.

His laughter echoed around the tunnels, and seemed to push the dread away, and

Erin smiled. She concentrated on using the pole as he chattered away, and gradually her worry faded. When she looked back at Connor, he was still gripping the sides of the boat, and Erin chuckled to herself.

After a while she saw a light ahead, which eventually became the end of the tunnel, and they emerged into warm morning sunlight on a small stream running through a wood. A little further on was a small wooden jetty.

"That's us," said Drun. He took the pole, skilfully brought the barge alongside, then leapt ashore and fastened a rope.

"Where are we?" asked Connor, looking around.

"Not far from where we need to be," said Drun.

Connor frowned. "Yes, but—"

"Up there," said Creedy curtly, and pointed to a small path.

It was old, overgrown and covered in mud and leaves, but Erin could see that underneath it was solid stone in large neat slabs. They took their bags and followed the path.

The woods were nice. Birds sang in the trees, and Erin realised how much she missed them. The Guild Hall was wonderful, but it had no wildlife. And out here there was a breeze, and the *swish* of leaves. As she walked, she found herself standing taller, breathing deeper.

Drun glanced across at her and smiled. "Aye," he murmured. "Good, ain't it?"

They reached the top of the hill and looked across another valley. The path led to a gateway in front of a line of tall trees. They followed Drun to the gate.

"What is this place?" asked Connor. Stone pillars stood on each side, and the gates were old wrought iron. A mark was carved into the stone on one side – three vertical lines, an old sign Erin had seen before.

"Dragon-made," said Connor softly to himself.

Where are we? asked Rockhammer's voice. *It feels ... nice.*

A woman in a dark-green robe walked down the driveway towards them, her feet crunching on the gravel with a pleasing sound.

"Hail!" called Drun cheerfully, and the figure waved. She pulled back her hood, and Erin and Connor gasped. It was Berin!

Only not quite, Erin realised after a moment. This woman's face was ruddier, warmed and windswept by a life of working outside, and she had rough gardener's hands. But her eyes were the same, and the smiling face. Round her neck was a blue stone, like the one on Berin's staff.

"Hello," she said, and her voice was like Berin's, too. "You must be Erin and Connor." She nodded to them. "My name is Hanna. Welcome to Stillness."

THE SOLACE
STONE

"My sister told me you were coming," said Hanna, as they walked up the drive.

"Your sister is the Lady Berin?" asked Connor, and Hanna nodded.

"So is this a part of the Guild?" Erin asked.

Connor made a face. "It's supposed to be *secret*!" he hissed.

Hanna smiled. "It's all right. There are no secrets here. In fact, once we are beyond these trees, your dragons can join you if they wish."

Erin and Rockhammer

They passed through a line of tall, graceful willow trees and found themselves in a beautiful garden. Flowers of all kinds and colours covered the gentle slopes, more than Erin had ever seen, in curves that seemed somehow both created and natural.

It wasn't like the formal, neat gardens at the palace back in Rivven, where every row was regimented and controlled. This seemed free and relaxed.

Beyond it was a large timber-framed house, which was nestled into the hillside behind it. Like the garden it seemed somehow half made, half grown. The wood was neat but not smoothed off, keeping the knots and whorls of its natural shape. Ivy and other climbing plants grew up and around it, and tiny white flowers peeked out from under the eaves.

Erin and Rockhammer were still connected, and now he drifted into view next to her. He always seemed so colossal in the Guild Hall. Sometimes it felt to Erin like there was no space for him to be. But out here he seemed to fit the open air.

"Ahhhh…" he growled softly. "I *like* this place!"

Erin nodded cautiously. "Hmm."

Lightspirit appeared next to Connor and sniffed around, nodding to herself.

Hanna led them inside, into a hallway formed of wooden beams and soft white plastered walls. It had clearly been built to suit dragons – the ceilings were high and the corridors wide enough even for Rockhammer.

"This is your room, Erin," said Hanna.

Erin peered inside. The room was simple

but cosy. There was a narrow bed, a dresser with a bowl of water for washing, and a vase of flowers. The window looked out to the garden.

"Connor, you're next door," said Hannah. "Make yourselves comfortable, and when you are ready come and join us for lunch. You'll find us back along the hall." She continued down the corridor with Drun and Creedy.

Connor entered his room. He didn't speak to Erin, and shut his door.

Erin stepped into her little room. There was just enough space for Rockhammer, but now he loomed, big and awkward, and after a moment he faded again.

It's a nice room, came his voice in her head.

Erin nodded. She sat on the bed, looked out of the window, and bit her lip. The room *was* nice. The lodge was nice. Hanna seemed nice. But still, she would rather be back at the Guild Hall. She didn't trust new things or places. She liked things to stay as they were, where she knew the rules of how things were. She liked to be with her friend Mira. Little tremors of worry started in her stomach.

But the sunlight, the garden and the solid wooden beams of her room were all calming. And there was something else about this place, in the air. She concentrated on just breathing in and out, and after a while she felt better.

And *hungry*, she realised.

On the other side of the hall was a long dining room, and when Erin arrived, the others were already there. Hanna and Drun smiled at her. Creedy gave her a thin nod. Connor ignored her. The table was spread with fruit, slices of cheese and ham, fresh bread, tomatoes and salad.

"Help yourself," said Hanna, and Erin dived in. After two enormous sandwiches of three types of cheese, *and* ham, plus a sweet crunchy apple, she felt much better.

"How was that?" asked Hanna.

"Good!" said Erin. She stifled a small burp, and Hanna chuckled.

"Well," she said, "if everyone's finished, there's something I'd like to show you."

She led them from the table and along another corridor, then down a set of steps to a plain wooden door. Hanna touched the stone on her necklace, and it glowed a soft blue. The door opened, and they entered.

They were in a wide chamber with a high ceiling. Rockhammer, still connected, appeared next to her and looked around. There were no windows – instead, light came from soft glowing globes, like the ones back at the Guild Hall. In the centre of the room was a wooden box on a stand. Its lid was open, and it was lined with silk.

Sitting inside the box was a jewel about the

size of Erin's thumb. It was milky white, like a pearl, and seemed to shine from within, a gentle white light.

And as Erin looked at it, she felt that everything – everything in the world – would be all right.

"It's beautiful," whispered Rockhammer, peering at it. "Erin, it's so ... *calm*."

Connor and Lightspirit were gazing at it, too. Connor's face, usually rather sharp, looked softer. Beside them, Drun was smiling as if meeting an old friend. Only Creedy still seemed like himself, careful and serious.

"This is the heart of Stillness," said Hanna.

"What is it?" breathed Erin.

"It is the Solace Stone," said Hanna. "It

creates calm. It gives us space to think."
She looked at Erin. "In this place, you can
take the time to relax and start again. Find
yourself when you are lost."

Erin gazed at the stone. She realised that for
the first time in forever she wasn't … *anxious*.
She wasn't worrying about Connor, or about
leaving the Guild, or saying the wrong thing.
She wasn't worrying about *worrying*. The
clean soft light passed through her and took
it all away.

"This is the heart of Stillness," said Hanna
again. "And while you are here it will help
you."

That night Erin slept well, and she awoke to

the smell of flowers, the sound of birdsong and the glow of golden morning light. She looked up at the ceiling and smiled. The only thing missing was Rockhammer. When Rockhammer and Erin were connected, the dragon could come and go into her world, fading in or out, staying in touch. But when she slept, the connection was lost.

She got up, dressed and walked out into the garden. To her surprise Drun was there already, tending a fire in a small stone pit.

He looked up at her and beamed. "Morning, miss! Got us ready for summoning. Shall we?"

Erin grinned. "Thanks, Drun."

He sat cross-legged on one side of the

small fire, and Erin sat on the other side. The grass was cool and still slightly damp from morning dew, but in a nice fresh way.

"Now," he said. "You know what to do, eh?"

Erin felt suddenly anxious. "You won't leave me to do it myself, will you?"

But he shook his head. "Don't you worry, miss. We'll work up to that another time."

Erin gazed into the flames, letting herself relax, and thinking lazily of Rockhammer, and soon she felt the connection, and saw two eyes, brown and glinting.

"Easy,"

murmured Drun. Erin let the connection grow. She felt the same worry as before, though it seemed weaker today. She almost thought she could…

"You do it," she said suddenly, and Drun completed the magic.

Behind her, Erin sensed the huge shape of Rockhammer, and smiled. "Hey, Rocky," she murmured, feeling his hot breath on her neck.

"Hello, Erin," he growled back.

Drun stood and stretched. "You nearly managed yourself that time."

Erin nodded. "Nearly."

"One day," said Drun. "We've got plenty of time. You can do it."

And for once Erin believed he might be right.

"Well," said Rockhammer, taking a deep breath of the fresh air, "what shall we do today?"

CONTROL

Life at Stillness was easy.

Every morning Erin stepped out into the garden to find Drun, and they summoned Rockhammer. Sometimes Drun suggested Erin take the last step, but she always resisted. Still – one day, perhaps?

Then Rockhammer faded away, keeping their connection so Erin could still feel his presence in her mind, as she went for her morning run through the woods.

DRAGON STORM

This had been Daisy's idea, back at the Guild. "Running's good for you," she'd said. "It builds muscles, improves your lungs, makes your heart strong. But also, it helps you relax. When you're running, all you have to do is put one foot in front of the other. It helps you burn off nervous energy. It puts your worries aside."

Erin wasn't convinced. Back at the Guild it had seemed that, no matter how far she ran, her worries were always waiting for her when she got back. But she did like the breeze on her skin and the good sort of tiredness in her legs, so every day she ran a long circuit round the lodge, into the woods on either side, along rabbit tracks and ancient byways.

Erin and Rockhammer

After her run, she helped Drun prepare supplies for the Guild, or worked with Hanna in the garden. She didn't see Connor or Creedy much, except at mealtimes. They were researching, poring through ancient books and papers held at the lodge. It was something Connor loved but Erin hated, and no one suggested she help.

Erin and Connor didn't talk much. She knew he'd been cross to begin with, thinking he was getting punished because of her. And that made her cross, because it had all been his fault! But, as the days passed, it didn't seem to matter so much. One morning, Erin nodded to him, and he nodded back. Hanna saw it and beamed.

DRAGON STORM

The calm around the lodge was like falling asleep after a busy, pleasing day. Rockhammer loved exploring the gardens, scaring the rabbits, looking for other creatures.

And Erin felt … happy.

On the fourth day, Erin thought she saw something on her run.

She was on the last climb back up to the lodge, on a twisting half-track. It was hard work and her lungs were burning, and the sun was flickering through the trees, when suddenly she saw a glint of silver.

She stopped, panting, and peered into the wood. There was nothing there, but she'd been sure she'd seen something. Silver, or steel, shining against something black, perhaps?

"Hello?" she called. "Is someone there?"

Nothing. The breeze was still shaking the leaves, breaking the morning sunlight into shimmering shapes.

What's up? asked Rockhammer.

"I'm not sure," she murmured.

Her skin prickled, tension running up her arms like electricity. She shivered. After a while, she shook her head and carried on running. She ran quickly, feeling the gap behind her back as if someone was about to leap at her, but nobody did.

Back at the lodge, Drun and Hanna weren't around, so Erin went to the library where Creedy and Connor worked. Creedy was there, surrounded by ancient books, muttering to himself. The book in front of him had an ancient drawing of the Solace Stone, with tiny written comments.

"Mr Creedy?"

He started and looked up in surprise. One hand covered the book. "I'm busy," he said in a flat voice.

"Yes, sir. Only…" Erin hesitated. "Um. I don't know, but … I thought I saw something in the woods."

Creedy gazed at her. He closed the book and sat back. "'Something'? What? A squirrel? A tree? An interesting leaf?"

Erin's cheeks flushed. "Someone," she said. "Someone wearing black and silver. Just for a moment, I mean, I could be wrong. But..." She trailed off.

He frowned. "And you're sure?" he asked at last.

Was she sure? The sunlight had been flickering, she'd been running hard... "No," she said awkwardly. "But I thought..."

"Hmm." Creedy shrugged. "Well. Thank you."

He leaned forward and opened another book. After a moment, he looked up.

"Anything else?"

"Um. No, sir."

He waved a hand. "Shoo."

Erin felt cross, with Creedy and with herself. Had she really seen something? Probably not. She was just worrying over nothing. And now Creedy thought she was a fool. She walked through the gardens and Rockhammer appeared beside her.

"He's so *mean*!" she said.

"I could eat him," said Rockhammer. "Would that help?"

Erin laughed. "Yeah. Chomp him up!"

"Bite his head off!" roared Rockhammer.

Erin snorted and felt better. They found

Hanna working on the roses, cutting off the older flowers with a pair of sharp blades. As they approached, Hanna turned and smiled.

"Good morning, Erin. How are you today?"

Erin tried to forget about Creedy, and smiled. "Good, thank you," she said. "What are you doing?"

"Deadheading," said Hanna. "It sounds rather awful, doesn't it?"

Erin thought about Creedy and exchanged a look with Rockhammer. She giggled. "A bit."

"It's to help the new flowers bloom," said Hannah. "Gardens can't stay perfect. You have to keep working at them." She smiled.

"I loved helping in the garden when I was a girl. Berin was always inside with a book, but I never could read like her. The words always seemed to move around when I tried. We were very different, and we fought so much!" She laughed and stripped some old leaves. "Is that why you and Connor argue, do you think?"

"No, it's because he's *mean*!" snapped Erin. "He's always making fun of me!" She felt the usual rush of anger, but not as strong. Out here, in the sunshine, with the effects of the Solace Stone around them, it seemed less real. Rockhammer rubbed his head against hers, and she sighed.

"It's not just that," she admitted. "I get

… scared, sometimes. And angry – *really* angry. Like I can't control it. Sometimes I worry there's … I don't know." She looked down. "Something wrong with me," she whispered.

"Well, *that's* not true!" said Rockhammer sharply.

Hanna snipped another rose. "I agree with Rockhammer, my dear," she said mildly. "You strike me as rather wonderful." She stood up straight. "There are things you may need a little help with, like everyone.

They're different for each person. Sometimes they can be strengths. Sometimes the strength comes from not letting them stop you."

She smiled and continued. "Berin and I don't argue so much these days. And one thing we certainly agree on is this: you are a good, strong person, Erin. You are brave. You are a *dragonseer*."

"Then why did she send me away?"

"She didn't!" said Hanna. "This is part of the Guild, just like the Hall. But here you can take a step aside. Get your strength back. Yes?"

Erin listened to the birdsong and felt the sun on her face. "It's easier when I'm here," she admitted.

"So. Take as long as you need. You can help me with the weeding."

Erin smiled. "Sure."

Erin thought about it the next morning. It had felt good to say it. Scary but good. And life *was* easier here. She started to wonder if she wanted to leave at all. Perhaps she could stay and look after the garden with Hanna?

Drun summoned Rockhammer, and Erin went for her run through the woods again. She peered around as she ran, glaring into the trees and bushes as if daring someone to appear, but there was nothing. She felt the breath in her lungs and the thud of her feet on the ground, and gradually relaxed.

DRAGON STORM

Back at the lodge, Drun had gone. Hanna wasn't around either.

Erin drank a long cup of water, and frowned. The building felt curiously quiet.

What's wrong, Erin? asked Rockhammer's voice, and he shimmered into view beside her.

"I don't know…" said Erin. She looked around, and then stopped. "Rocky, look!" she whispered.

There were muddy footprints in the hallway. But they weren't Hanna's, and not Drun's either. These were large marks left by heavy square-toed boots.

Soldiers' boots.

SOLDIERS

"Soldiers' boots," whispered Erin. "Rocky, there are soldiers here!"

Rockhammer growled and his spiked ridge stood up. The footprints led along the corridor past their bedrooms. Erin's heart was beating fast, but she stayed silent and crept after them. Rockhammer followed, moving surprisingly quietly for such a large creature. At the end of the corridor was Hanna's study, and Erin paused. The door was open a crack, and angry voices came from inside. She held her breath and peered through the crack.

There were at least a dozen soldiers. They wore black uniforms with silver flames embroidered on the sleeves, and carried steel swords. Two of them were holding Hanna, and two were holding Drun.

Before them was a woman in a similar uniform but with stripes on her sleeve. She had high cheekbones, a jutting chin and long red hair. She seemed to be in charge.

"Who else is here?" she was demanding.

Hanna and Drun glared at her but said nothing. The woman nodded to the soldiers holding Drun, and they held their swords

against his throat.

The woman turned to Hanna. "Tell me." Her voice was smooth and confident.

Hanna sighed. "No one."

"No staff?" asked the woman. "No servants?" She gestured to Drun. "Who's this?"

"He's my gardener," said Hanna. "The other staff are at home today; they won't be in till later." She shook her head. "This is a mistake," she said quietly. "There are no riches here, no money or jewels. Whatever you're looking for—"

"You know why we're here," interrupted the woman. "There is an artefact hidden here at Stillness." She lifted her head, as if tasting the air. "I can *feel* it." She looked back at Hanna. "We're here for the Solace Stone. *You* will take us to it. If you don't…" She lifted a finger, and the soldiers near Drun raised their swords again.

"Don't do it, Hanna!" bellowed Drun, ignoring their blades.

But Hanna's expression fell. "Very well," she muttered. "I will take you to it, on condition that no one is harmed."

The woman smiled, cold and sharp. "We'll all go."

Almost too late, Erin realised the soldiers were heading for the corridor! She heaved Rockhammer away and found the door to her room, and they hid inside just in time.

Rockhammer filled the room, squeezing Erin into a corner. She felt a shiver of panic rising inside her and tried to keep her breathing smooth and calm.

The soldiers clattered past their door and beyond, and then the corridor was quiet.

"Those were the soldiers from the palace!" growled Rockhammer. "The ones we saw before, the Silver Guards!"

Erin nodded. She was sweating. Despite the calming effects of the Solace Stone, her heart was pounding.

"What should we do?" asked Rockhammer.

Erin bit her lip. "I don't know…"

But, squaring her shoulders, she opened the door and slipped down the corridor after them.

They sneaked back to the main hall, and downstairs to where the Stone was kept. This corridor was too narrow for Rockhammer, so he shimmered out of sight, but Erin could still feel his presence in her mind, worried and angry and ready to fight. Erin crept forward again.

The soldiers were there. They seemed to be searching for something. The woman was there, too, standing beside the Stone, glaring at Hanna.

"Don't lie to me!" she snapped.

Hanna's eyes were dark with anger, but her voice was steady. "I don't know what you're talking about."

"My orders," said the woman, "are to retrieve the Stone and the Book of Solace. *Where is the book?*"

What's the Book of Solace? asked Rockhammer.

Erin shook her head. She had no idea. From the blank look on Hanna's face, she didn't seem to know either.

The woman cursed. "How do you control it?" she asked. "How do you make it work? How do you *stop* it working?"

"It's not a machine!" said Hanna sharply. "You can't just turn it on or off! It's the Solace Stone. It gives solace. That's what it *does*."

The woman scowled, chewing her lip.

She glared at the box and picked it up, and seemed surprised at the weight of it. She inspected the lid and nodded.

"Interesting," she said. "Why would someone line a box with *lead*, I wonder?" Hanna didn't answer, but the woman smiled. "Perhaps I can guess. You can't turn the Stone's powers off ... but perhaps you could block its effects? Say ... like *this*?"

And she closed the heavy lid with a snap.

The pearly white light stopped. The calmness that had spread out from the Solace Stone stopped. And suddenly...

DRAGON STORM

Suddenly Erin felt *everything*.

Panic crashed over her like a wave. The effects of the Solace Stone vanished, and all her worry and chaos and anxiety returned to her in a moment. She gasped, hardly even able to breathe. Her body seized up, ready to fight, or run, or lash out, and she felt sick.

We have to go! hissed Rockhammer's voice. *Erin, we have to GO!*

She stumbled back along the corridor. What was she going to *do*? Drun and Hanna were captured, there were soldiers in the lodge, they had the Solace Stone—

Come on! said Rockhammer. Even inside her head, his voice was a snarl, ready for a fight.

Erin tried to think. "Creedy!" she croaked. She staggered back up the steps and towards the library.

Erin could hardly see for panic. She tried to control it. She tried to imagine this was just a training fight at the Guild. But Rockhammer's presence in her mind was dangerous and savage, and now Erin remembered her one great fear.

"Wait!" she called.

What? came Rockhammer's voice. *You want us to fight? Should we fight them? I can! I can fight them!*

"No," she whispered. "Rocky, I'm sorry…"

What for?

"For this."

She broke the connection.

She felt his astonishment. *Why did you do that?!* he had time to say, before he was gone.

"I'm sorry, Rocky," whispered Erin again. "I'll explain later, I *promise*."

She stumbled on through the lodge, feeling the panic rise.

CHAOS

"Mr Creedy!" called Erin, bursting into the library. "Mr Creedy, help us!"

She stopped. Creedy wasn't there. There was just Connor, working. He looked up and scowled.

"What do *you* want?" he asked in a hostile voice.

Erin stared around wildly. *No, no, no*, she thought. Little bolts of electricity raced up and down her arms, and her stomach ached.

She was close to panic.

"Where's Creedy?" she demanded. "There are soldiers here in the lodge! Where *is* he?"

Connor stood. "What? What are you talking about?"

She tried to stay calm. "Remember the Silver Guards we saw at the palace?" she panted. "With the black uniforms and the flames on their sleeves? They're *here*! Downstairs! They've got Hanna and Drun, and the Solace Stone, and they've shut the box; it's not working any more – can't you feel it?"

Connor hesitated. Then he nodded. "Well, don't *panic*, anyway," he said scornfully.

Erin's hands balled into fists. "Where's

Creedy?" she asked through gritted teeth, trying to hold back the chaos in her mind.

"He left a few minutes ago to get something." Connor rubbed his chin. "And you're sure?"

"Of course I am!" snapped Erin.

"Yes, all right, calm down."

"Don't tell me to calm down!" she shouted. "I hate it when you tell me to calm down!"

She raced back through the lodge, searching for Creedy. Where could he be? At last she heard a sound from one of the rooms and opened the door—

She gasped and staggered back.

In front of her was a soldier. He was tall, in black and silver, and his face was grim, but he seemed as surprised as she was.

Connor crashed into the back of Erin, looked up, and yelped.

The soldier looked from Erin to Connor. "What are you kids doing here?" he asked in a rough voice.

Erin swallowed. "I…"

"Do you know this place?" he demanded. "Where's the library?"

They said nothing, staring at him. The soldier's face darkened in anger. "Tell me!" he snarled, and stepped forward…

Erin charged at him.

"YAAAAAAAARGH!" she screamed.

The soldier stepped back in surprise and fumbled for his sword, but she smashed into

him, almost knocking him off his feet. But
not quite – he shoved her back, swinging a
wild blow that whistled past her ear as she
ducked.

"Stop that, you little brat!" he roared, and
tried to grab her in a bear hug. She collapsed,
slipping through his arms, and swung her
legs round, kicking with both her feet against

one knee as hard as she could. He swore, stumbled and crashed to the floor. His head smacked against the wall as he landed, and he stopped moving.

Erin stared at him, panting. Beside her, Connor looked stunned. She scrambled to her feet. "Come on!" she shouted, dragging Connor down the corridor.

Behind them, she heard the soldier groan and start to get up.

Erin felt like she was on fire. Adrenaline pounded through her like steel pins pulling and pushing. She felt sick and like she was watching herself from above. Panic raced through her. All she could think to do was get away. A door opened ahead of them and she skidded to a halt, her blood pounding in her ears.

It was Creedy, entering the lodge through the back door, walking softly and peering around.

"Mr Creedy!" called Connor.

Creedy saw them. For a moment he looked astonished, before his face closed into its usual grim expression. "What is it, boy?" he growled.

"There are soldiers!" gasped Erin. "Downstairs! They've got Hanna and Drun! They've got the *Solace Stone*! What are you doing?

Where *were* you?"

Creedy hesitated. "I went for a walk," he said at last. "What are you talking about?"

"You said you were fetching a book," said Connor, surprised.

Erin stared at Creedy. A book? What was happening? The chaos was like wasps buzzing around her head. She couldn't think properly. Her temper was rising, her stomach ached and she wanted to lash out again, to get this energy out of her. And now, in the back of her mind, she could see two eyes, dragon eyes…

"What's going on?" she demanded. "You're lying! What book?"

Creedy blinked at her. "Calm down, girl."

"DON'T TELL ME TO CALM DOWN!" Erin screamed. "DON'T SAY THAT! DON'T – Oh no."

The room trembled. Creedy and Connor looked about them in alarm.

"What was that?" asked Connor, grabbing a table.

"No, no, no," moaned Erin.

The two eyes glared at her, furious and powerful, and she wrapped her arms round her head. "No, don't. Don't!"

"What are you talking about?" asked Creedy.

And then, in one moment, many things happened. The wooden ceiling beams above them buckled and snapped. The floor cracked open and gave way underneath them. The windows blew out in a shower of glass, and there was a noise like a hurricane in the room, and a glimpse of something fierce, and enormous, with huge spikes up its back, and razor-sharp claws and teeth. The last thing Erin saw was Rockhammer's face, wild, roaring…

The lodge collapsed. Something hit her head, and the world went dark.

BURIED

When Erin woke up, a dragon was glaring at her.

It was Lightspirit, Connor's dragon. Her face was scrunched into a frown, and her nose was twitching.

"She's awake," Lightspirit said, and moved away.

Erin sat up, and then clutched the back of her head. There was a lump the size of an egg there.

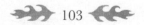

She looked around. It was dark. A single cracked globe lamp lay on the ground, still glowing but faint. Broken wooden beams lay at crazy angles around them, covered in plaster and smashed furniture. The falling debris seemed to have made a tiny cave around them.

Erin and Rockhammer

Connor came over and kneeled beside her. His face, clothes and hair were caked white in dust, like a ghost. "Are you OK?" he asked.

Erin felt the bruise on her head and winced, but nodded. "I think so." Her voice was a croak. "What happened?"

"The roof collapsed," said Connor. "And the floor. We've fallen into a cellar, I think. Something hit you on the head and knocked you out. Creedy as well."

He pointed to the side, and Erin saw Creedy. He was breathing but unconscious.

"It collapsed right where you two were standing," said Connor. "It's amazing we weren't crushed." His voice was hoarse and trembling.

"How long was I unconscious?" asked Erin.

"A few minutes," he said. "I heard people running. I think it was the soldiers leaving. I don't know what's happened to Drun and Hanna."

Erin and Rockhammer

Erin didn't want to move, but she forced herself to stand up. There was space for that at least.

"Is there any way out?"

Connor sighed. "No. Two of the main roof beams are on top of us. We can't possibly move them. Not even you, me and Lightspirit together."

He gave Erin a strange look. "What happened?"

"I don't know," said Erin, biting her lip and looking away. The ceiling had collapsed. The floor. And she'd seen something in the chaos. Something she knew...

"We have to get out," she said. She tried to move one of the wooden beams, but it was massive, too heavy to budge even a millimetre. "Can we make a lever?"

"I tried that," said Connor. "Maybe Rockhammer could help?"

Erin shook her head. "No."

He frowned. "Why not? He's strong."

"*I'm* strong!" snapped Lightspirit. She looked down. "I'm *quite* strong," she muttered.

"Rockhammer can't help us," said Erin. "I can't summon him myself. *You* know that. You're always *laughing* at me about it."

Connor looked slightly ashamed. "Yes, well. It's got to be worth a try, though, hasn't it?"

"I can't."

Erin and Rockhammer

"But I could help!" he protested. "And you said you managed once – you're always telling that story! About the very first time you met him, when you summoned him, after your house had been hit by lightning! When it…"

He stopped. "When it collapsed," he said slowly. His eyes widened. "When your house collapsed."

Erin sank to the ground and covered her face. "It's my fault," she groaned. "It's all my fault!"

"Erin," asked Lightspirit in a soft voice, "what's going on?"

"Don't you *see*?" wailed Erin. She waved a hand around. "*This* is why I can't summon him! *This* is what happens!"

Connor stared at her. "No," he said, shaking his head. "No, that's not right. I mean… I mean…"

"*Yes*." She burst into tears. Oh, *Rocky*. She wanted to see him more than anything. He was her best friend, and the one person she *couldn't* see. "Rocky!"

Something touched her knee. She looked up to see Lightspirit patting her with one paw. The dragon glared at Connor and tilted her head, and he sat awkwardly next to Erin.

"Um … hey," he said softly. "It's OK."

They sat quietly. For once Connor didn't talk, and Erin was grateful.

"I get … anxious," she said at last.

Connor shrugged. "Well, we all get scared sometimes, right? I mean—"

"Shh!" said Lightspirit, and he fell quiet.

"Not like that," said Erin. "Like … small things. Things that shouldn't matter. I worry. I don't like change. It's OK when I'm

, I don't mind that. But sometimes I get anxious, and I … panic. It's hard to breathe, I feel sick, and it just *happens*. And people say 'calm down', but I *can't*. And sometimes it gets really bad, and I lash out, or say horrible things, or…"

She sank her head against her knees.

"The first time I met Rockhammer, I was upset. I was in a foster home, and everything was new, and I was worried, and I got … *angry*. My foster parents were upset, and I thought they'd send me back to the orphanage, and I got more upset, and sick, and I … I saw these eyes, like inside my head. The more upset I got, the more I saw them, and then Rockhammer appeared, but he was *wild*. He destroyed everything – my room, the house, everything!"

"You said he saved you," said Connor.

Erin shook her head. "I don't know. The house collapsed, but somehow no one was hurt. Maybe that was him. But he caused it!"

She sighed. "The Solace Stone made things better, but then that woman closed the box, and it was worse than ever. And then Creedy wasn't there, and none of it made sense, and the f-fight, and I was so *scared*, and Rocky came back…" She shook her head.

They sat together in the almost dark, Lightspirit with her paw on Erin's knee,

Connor silent.

"He's not normally like that," said Connor at last, frowning.

"He's very annoying," said Lightspirit, sniffing. She shook her head. "But he's not wild."

"He gets like that when I lose control," said Erin.

"Hmm," said Lightspirit thoughtfully. "Perhaps it's not him? A dragonseer has tremendous power. They can reach across worlds! Perhaps that power is getting distorted somehow? So Rockhammer is coming through ... different?"

Erin nodded. "You mean it's me," she said miserably.

"Well, that's not—"

"It *is*, though," insisted Erin. "It happens when I summon him. I'm not a proper dragonseer. There's something *wrong* with me."

Lightspirit blinked in astonishment. "What rubbish. You're perfectly normal!" She shrugged. "For a human anyway."

"It doesn't sound right to me either," said Connor. He scratched his head. "I mean, how can you not be proper? You have a dragon – you *are* a dragonseer, Erin." He frowned. "Maybe it's just that every time you've summoned him before now, you've been really upset. Like … out of control?" He nodded. "If you summon him now, while you're calm, it might work."

"Are there things you do to stay calm?" asked Lightspirit.

Erin tried to think. "Daisy says to concentrate on breathing," she said at last. "When I get panicked. It helps sometimes." She shook her head. "But I *can't*. I'm not strong enough."

Connor chuckled. "You're *very* strong," he said. "Stronger than me for sure."

"That's not what I mean."

"I know. But you are. And faster. And people like you, and you're good at dragon riding, and flying, and running…" Connor hesitated. Then he said, "You're quite intimidating really."

Erin blinked. "What?"

He blushed. "Well, you're so *great* at everything. And you always run towards danger; you never seem scared!"

"I'm scared all the time!" exclaimed Erin.

"Then you're brave," said Connor. "Because you do stuff even when you're scared. You saved us from that soldier. You're strong. I mean ... you're strong inside."

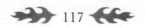

Erin didn't feel strong. She felt weak. She worried when no one else did. She overreacted, lost control. But then she remembered what Hanna had said, about everyone having things they needed help with…

Sometimes the strength comes from not letting them stop you.

She tried to remember how it felt when she charged into a fight. There was danger, but also something *wonderful* about running towards something that terrified you. Could she do that? Could she run towards this? Could she do it despite her fear?

"All right," she said finally. Her voice

cracked, and she coughed. "All right. Let's do it.

"Let's summon Rockhammer."

SUMMONING

Erin and Connor sat cross-legged, facing each other.

"There's no fire," said Erin. "I can't summon Rockhammer without a fire."

"You don't really need the fire," said Connor.

"But I do!" she protested. "I need it or I can't summon him! I need it!"

He opened his mouth, and for a moment – a furious, sharp moment – Erin thought he was going to tell her to calm down. But then he closed his mouth and nodded again.

"Let's just start small," he said gently, "and see what happens. And if it doesn't work, we'll try something else. How does that sound?"

Erin hesitated. "All right." She tried to feel confident. "I'll try."

"So –" Connor frowned, thinking – "when I connect with Lightspirit, I remember all the things I like about her. You could try that?"

Erin nodded. She closed her eyes and imagined Rockhammer.

It was difficult. She loved Rockhammer, but so often she felt guilty about him. She remembered the foster home collapsing around her, and how terrified her foster parents had been. She remembered when Malik had come along, how relieved they'd been to make her someone else's problem. Because that's what she was – a problem. Because *she* was the problem. Because there was something *wrong* with her…

Her mind whirled in a loop of horrible thoughts. About every time she'd shouted, or lashed out, or lost control. She couldn't stop. She couldn't stop *thinking* about it—

"Steady," murmured Connor. Erin realised he was holding her hand. It made her think of Rockhammer resting his paw against her. And then she remembered flying, and leaning against Rockhammer's warm belly, sharing a joke with him. So often, she realised, Rockhammer was the one who calmed her down. He reassured her when she was upset, distracted her when she was becoming obsessed… When she thought about him, she often remembered disaster, but actually he was a *strength*.

As she thought this, she saw something in her mind. Two soft brown eyes, dragon eyes, and somehow she knew that the face behind those eyes was smiling…

She gasped. "I can see him!"

Connor nodded. "Can you summon him?"

Erin felt a jolt of fear. But she thought about what Connor had said. *You're brave. You always run towards danger.*

She thought: *I run towards the things that scare me. I get anxious. I worry. I panic. But I'm strong. These things won't stop me...*

She screwed her eyes closed, ignoring the tremble in her hands, ignoring the sick knot in her stomach, ignoring the sharp jolts of adrenaline running along her nerves. *They won't stop me.* Come on, Rocky...

She heard Lightspirit gasp.

"Hello, Erin," said Rockhammer, and she opened her eyes to see him in front of her, huge and powerful, smiling with his enormous mouth and with his big brown eyes.

"*Rocky!*" Erin leapt to her feet and wrapped her arms round his neck. "Oh, Rocky, you're *here!*"

He rested his head gently against hers. "I'm here."

"It was me," she half sobbed. "It wasn't your fault; it was *me*."

But he smiled even wider. "It's you *and* me, Erin. You're my human, and I'm your dragon. It's you *and* me always."

She hugged him tight, but then pulled away. "Rocky, we need your help. We're trapped, can you get us out?"

Rockhammer looked at the broken cross-beams and destruction. The space suddenly felt very tiny with him there. "Hmm," he said. He sniffed at Creedy, still unconscious. "Hmm."

"What do you think?" asked Connor. "Can

you help?"

"Of course!" said Rockhammer, pushing his chest out proudly. "But I don't know how stable this is. If I move those beams…"

He tapped the wood with his claw. It moved, but pieces fell around it, dust and small stones, and there was an ominous rumble. Connor, Erin and Lightspirit ducked.

"Hmm," said Rockhammer again.

There was another noise from outside, like something shifting.

"Did you hear that?" asked Connor.

"Hello?" called Erin. "Is someone there?"

They listened, and then, faintly, they heard a voice. "Miss, is that you?"

"Drun!" cheered Erin. "Drun, it's us, we're

here! And Mr Creedy, too!"

"Hold tight!" shouted Drun's muffled voice. "We're coming for you!"

There was a sound of moving rubble, coming closer, someone digging towards them, and Erin and Connor grinned at each other. But Rockhammer looked worried, and Erin realised more plaster was falling inside their tiny space, too. The cross-beams trembled.

"Wait!" called Connor. "It's not stable!"

"We're almost there!" came Drun's voice.

"No, *wait*!" shouted Erin. The sounds stopped, but the beams were still shaking.

Rockhammer looked around him, and gave a deep low growl. "Hmmmmmm…"

He ducked his head and seemed to loom even larger in the space. The ridge on his back stood up.

"Rocky, what's happening?" asked Erin nervously.

"I think he's getting his powers!" murmured Lightspirit. "He's getting them now!"

"But what can he do?" asked Connor. "Hammer the beams away? It's too dangerous!"

More debris was falling from above, bricks, stones and more dust. The main cross-beam shuddered and groaned under the weight. "It's going to break!" shouted Erin. "Cover your head! Watch out for bricks! Watch out—"

The beam split with a sound like lightning! The ceiling above them collapsed, and Erin clamped her arms over her head and screamed…

Then she stopped.

Nothing was happening. She peered up to see Rockhammer, his eyes closed, standing in the middle of the space. He seemed to be humming, very quietly but very deeply. And above him the ceiling … was still there. It wasn't moving, though nothing was holding it up any more. The broken cross-beam was holding, though it couldn't possibly be. Around them, bricks and stones hung in the air, gently bobbing. Dust shimmered in the light of the broken globe.

"What is this?" breathed Lightspirit, gazing up.

Erin gazed at Rockhammer. He seemed to be surrounded by a soft golden glow. "It's Rocky," she murmured. "This is his power, I think. He's stopping the ceiling from collapsing."

Connor stared at the bricks. "How?" he whispered.

"He's keeping it stable somehow," said Erin. She smiled. "Holding everything together... Do you see? *This* is his power – not to destroy, but to *stop things falling apart*..."

Connor suddenly laughed. "I thought he would be like a hammer," he said. "But he's a *rock*!"

"He's *my* rock," said Erin proudly.

Erin and Rockhammer

A scraping sound came from one corner, and a light appeared.

"Miss!" shouted Drun. His face was covered in dust, and he had a rope tied around his middle. "Thank goodness I found ye. Is everyone all right?"

"We're all right," said Connor, "but Mr Creedy's unconscious."

"Let's get everyone out of here before the whole place collapses!" said Drun.

Erin smiled. "It's OK," she said. "Rockhammer's got it."

Rockhammer, still humming, opened one eye and smiled back.

 # BETTER

Erin and Connor crawled out through the tiny gap and found themselves in the room they'd seen before, the one that had held the Solace Stone. Drun followed them, pulling Creedy, who moaned slightly and seemed to be waking up.

Hanna was there, and when she saw them, her face lit up.

"Oh, children!" she cried, and hugged them both. "Oh, thank goodness you're safe!"

Erin and Rockhammer

"Rockhammer saved us," said Connor.

Erin looked back through the tunnel to see Rockhammer, still humming, holding the ruins of cross-beams and rubble together. Lightspirit sat next to him.

"Stay back!" called Lightspirit. The two dragons nodded to each other, and faded out of sight, though Erin could still feel her link with Rockhammer. The space shook, and then collapsed in a crash of destruction! The lodge trembled, and the globes above them swung back and forward, but then there was silence.

Rockhammer shimmered back into view beside her. "Erin!" he roared excitedly. "Did you see that?"

Erin laughed. "You saved us, Rocky! You did it!"

"*You* did it!" he exclaimed. "You summoned me!"

Erin laughed again and hugged him.

"I'm so sorry," she said to Hanna later.

They sat in the garden, listening to the birds singing and the bees buzzing from flower to flower. Behind them, Drun was organising repairs to the lodge, and Rockhammer was moving some of the larger pieces of rubble and wood. Creedy was watching from the side, sitting in a comfortable chair with bandages round his head. He seemed to be enjoying the sunshine – he was hardly scowling at all.

Hanna smiled. "There's nothing to apologise for. No one was seriously harmed. Mr Creedy is much better. All of this –" she waved an arm at the destruction – "is just things. Things can be fixed."

"But they took the Solace Stone," insisted Erin. "If I hadn't … reacted … we might have been able to stop them."

But Hanna shook her head. "That woman was dangerous, and not to be trifled with.

Erin and Rockhammer

I don't know who she was, or who sent her – but you would not have been able to stop her." Then she laughed. "But you should have seen them all scurry when the building collapsed! They'd planned to take us with them, but they ran instead."

"We've seen them before," said Erin. "When we were in the palace. We think they're some sort of secret army for King Godfic."

"Perhaps." Hanna's face became serious. "Something is happening, Erin. I don't know why they took the Solace Stone, but it must be important to them. To carry out a raid like this… Whoever is doing this, they're becoming bold. Soon we shall have to face them." She softened. "But not today."

"What will you do if they come back?" asked Erin, worried, but Hanna smiled.

"I doubt they will," she said. "They have what they wanted. But if they do… This place has its own defences, should we need them." She touched the blue stone on her necklace, and it shone brightly, and her eyes sparked. "Next time we'll be prepared."

The barge slipped through the dark water as they made their way back through the tunnel to the Guild Hall. Drun and Erin worked the poles, as before, and Connor sat scrunched at one end, holding on tight to the sides. Creedy was stretched out, grumbling every time the boat shifted or water splashed up. He was almost entirely better but still complained about his head, and their steering, and the splashing, and anything else. Erin found him a lot less intimidating now.

They arrived at the small dock to find Berin waiting for them. She gave them a warm smile and hugged them.

"We'll talk later," she said, "but for now, take it easy. It's good to see you both."

Connor and Erin helped unpack the boat and then made their way back upstairs, into the Hall.

It's good to be back, said Rockhammer's voice, and Erin grinned.

He appeared next to her and she patted his

side. "It's good to be home," she said.

Connor nodded. He seemed to be thinking about something. "What should we do about Creedy?" he asked at last.

Erin looked at him. "You mean…"

"He told Hanna he heard the soldiers, and went to explore," said Connor. "But he told me he was going to fetch something. And he told *you* he was taking a walk."

Erin shook her head. "It's strange. But I wasn't … thinking clearly. Maybe I misunderstood."

"Hmm." Connor walked on. "Why would they take the Solace Stone?"

Erin shrugged. "It's valuable, I suppose? It's magic…"

"Yes, but why now? It's been there for hundreds of years. And it's not *very* powerful – all it does is make things calm…"

"That's quite powerful," said Erin, smiling.

Connor frowned. "Hmm. Yes. Look, I, um…" He stopped. "I'm … uh…"

Beside him, Lightspirit appeared. "For heaven's sake *say* it," she snapped, and Connor blushed.

"I'm sorry," he said at last. "For making fun of you about summoning."

Erin smiled. "Thank you. I'm sorry too,

for getting angry. And for laughing at your sword fighting."

They walked on.

"I mean," said Erin, "for laughing at how *bad* your sword fighting is."

"Yes, I get it," said Connor.

"Your terrible, *terrible* sword fighting," she said, grinning. "I'm sorry for laughing at how *dreadful* it is, oh dear!"

He snorted. "All right, that's enough!"

"No, no!" Erin laughed. "Let me say sorry some more, for laughing at your dragon riding, too! And your running, and wrestling, and that time you dropped your shield on your foot—"

He punched her arm, and she punched

him back, but softly.

"So…" he said after a while, "are you …

better then? I mean, are you … fixed?"

Erin thought about how to answer.

"It doesn't work like that," she said gently.

"I get anxious. Sometimes I panic and lash out. Sometimes I get overwhelmed and angry for no reason. I thought the Solace Stone would fix it, but it can't, not really. It's part of who I am.

"But it doesn't *control* me. Some stuff is harder or scarier. But I'm still me. Some things are strengths, and some things make you strong when you don't let them stop you. When you run towards what scares you."

She hesitated. "Daisy asked if I wanted to take part in a sword-fighting contest in Strick. I said no before. I don't like going to new places. But maybe I should. I'm a bit … nervous."

"Huh." Connor thought for a while. Then

he said, "Well, they'll probably all be better than you anyway. You'll probably come last, right?"

Erin stared at him in shock. "What? Why would you say that?"

Connor smirked. "Imagine, *you* coming last in sword fighting! I'd love to see that. In fact…" He shrugged. "Maybe I'll come along too. Not to keep you company or anything. Just to, you know, watch you lose."

Erin looked at him, and eventually she grinned and rolled her eyes. "Well, if you *must*. Hey, you can carry my swords."

"No way!"

"Not strong enough, eh?"

He laughed.

"Hanna and Berin say something is coming," said Erin suddenly. "A crisis, Berin called it. Whatever King Godfic is planning, he's going to make his move soon."

Connor nodded. "Yeah. You scared?"

"A bit." Then she shrugged. "But you know what? If something *is* coming…"

Erin looked up at Rockhammer, who was walking alongside, and he gave her a huge fierce smile.

"We're ready for it," he growled.

EPILOGUE

"They suspect," said Creedy later.

He sat at his desk in his room in the Guild Hall, in the flickering glow of a small lamp. The room was normally tidy – Creedy hated mess – but now the desk was piled with scraps of paper and parchment, and ancient books lay scattered about. The books were covered in symbols and strange writing. Some showed drawings of the Solace Stone.

DRAGON STORM

What do you think they'll do? asked a dark voice. It was Nightwatcher, Creedy's own dragon. As she spoke, Creedy could see her eyes in his mind, red and fierce.

He scowled. "I don't know. The girl was confused. But the boy…" He stood and doused the lamp, then pulled aside the curtain over his small window. It was night-time, and the globes were dark. The young dragonseers were sitting round a campfire and Drun was telling them a story. Creedy could see Connor's face, sharp and watchful.

"The boy is clever," said Creedy. "He won't forget."

If he's clever, perhaps he can help us with our problem, said Nightwatcher.

Creedy hesitated. "Hmm," he said at last.

Perhaps we should let him know the truth.

"No." Creedy shook his head. "Not yet. But soon. In fact, I think…"

He let the curtain fall, and the room became dark.

"Soon *everyone* will know."

Look out for more books in
the Dragon Storm series:

CONNOR AND LIGHTSPIRIT

SKYE AND SOULSINGER